THE VOICE IMITATOR

TRANSLATED BY KENNETH J. NORTHCOTT

DESIGNED B

JESSICA HELFAND | WILLIAM DRENTTE

THOMAS BERNHARD

VOICE IMITATOR

THE UNIVERSITY OF CHICAGO PRESS
CHICAGO AND LONDON

THOMAS BERNHARD (1931–1989)

was an Austrian playwright, novelist, and poet. English translations of his works published by the University of Chicago Press include *Woodcutters* and *Wittgenstein's Nephew: A Friendship*, both translated by David McLintock; *Histrionics: Three Plays*, translated by Peter Jansen and Kenneth J. Northcott; *The Loser: A Novel*, translated by Jack Dawson; and *Yes*, translated by Ewald Osers.

The University of Chicago Press, Chicago 60637
The University of Chicago Press Ltd., London
©1997 by The University of Chicago

All rights reserved. Published 1997
Printed in the United States of America
06 05 04 03 02 01 00 99 98 97   1 2 3 4 5
ISBN 0-226-04401-7 (cloth)

Originally published as *Der Stimmenimitator*,
© Suhrkamp Verlag Frankfurt am Main 1978.

Library of Congress Cataloging-in-Publication Data

Bernhard, Thomas.
    [Stimmenimitator. English.]
    The voice imitator / Thomas Bernhard; translated by
  Kenneth J. Northcott.
        p. cm.
    ISBN 0-226-04401-7 (alk. paper)
    I. Northcott, Kenneth J. II. Title.
  PT2662.E7S713 1997
  833′.914—dc21

CONTENTS

104 STORIES

Near Oslo we met a man of about sixty who told us more about the old people's home than we already knew from reading Hamsun's accounts of the last year of his life, because he had been working in the home at precisely the time during which the greatest of Norwegian writers was living there. The man's taciturnity had attracted our attention in the inn near Oslo—usually so noisy on a Friday evening—where we were staying for several nights. After we had sat down at his table and introduced ourselves, we learned that the man had originally been a philosophy student and had, among other things, spent four years studying at Göttingen. We had taken him for a Norwegian ship's captain and had come to his table to hear some more about seafaring, not about philosophy, from which, indeed, we had fled north from Central Europe. But the man didn't bother us with philosophy and said he had actually given up philosophy overnight and put himself at the disposal of geriatrics at the age of twenty-seven. He said he did not regret his decision. He told us his first task had been to help an old man get out of bed, make the bed for him, and then put him back into it. The old man was Hamsun. He had looked after Hamsun every day for several months, had taken him out into the garden that lay behind the old people's home, and had gone to the village for him to buy the pencils that Hamsun used to write his last book. He was, he said, the first person to see Hamsun *dead*. In the nature of things, he said, he was not yet certain who Hamsun was when he pulled the sheet up over his face.

The voice imitator, who had been invited as the guest of the surgical society last evening, had declared himself—after being introduced in the Palais Pallavinci—willing to come with us to the Kahlenberg, where our house was always open to any artist whatsoever who wished to demonstrate his art there—not of course without a fee. We had asked the voice imitator, who hailed from Oxford in England but who had attended school in Landshut and had originally been a gunsmith in Berchtesgaden, not to repeat himself on the Kahlenberg but to present us something entirely different from what he had done for the surgical society; that is, to imitate quite different people from those he had imitated in the Palais Pallavinci, and he had promised to do this for us, for we had been enchanted with the program that he had presented in the Palais Pallavinci. In fact, the voice imitator did imitate voices of quite different people—all more or less well known—from those he had imitated before the surgical society. We were allowed to express our own wishes, which the voice imitator fulfilled most readily. When, however, at the very end, we suggested that he imitate his own voice, he said he could not do that.

Two philosophers, about whom more has been written than they themselves have published, who met again—after not seeing one another for decades—in, of all places, Goethe's house in Weimar, to which they had gone, in the nature of things, separately and from opposite directions—something that, since it was winter and consequently very cold, had presented the greatest difficulties to both of them—simply for the purpose of getting to know Goethe's habits better, assured each other, at this unexpected and for both of them painful meeting, of their mutual respect and admiration and at the same time told each other that, once back home, they would immerse themselves in each other's writings with the intensity appropriate to, and worthy of, those writings. When, however, one of them said he would give an account of his meeting in the Goethe House in the newspaper that was, in his opinion, the best and would do so, in the nature of things, in the form of a philosophical essay, the other immediately resisted the idea and characterized his colleague's intention as character assassination.

In Montreux, on Lake Geneva, we noticed a lady sitting on a park bench on the shore of the lake, who would, from time to time, on this same park bench, receive and then dismiss again the most diverse visitors, without moving a muscle. Twice a car stopped in front of her on the lake shore, and a young man in uniform got out, brought her the newspapers, and then drove off again; we thought it must be her private chauffeur. The lady was wrapped in several blankets, and we guessed her age to be well over seventy. Sometimes she would wave at a passerby. Probably, we thought, she is one of those rich and respectable Swiss ladies who live on Lake Geneva in the winter while their business is carried on in the rest of the world. The woman was, as we were soon informed, actually one of the richest and most respectable of the Swiss ladies who spend the winter on Lake Geneva; for twenty years she had been a paraplegic and had had her chauffeur drive her almost every day for those twenty years to the shore of Lake Geneva, had always had herself installed on the same bench, and had had the newspapers brought to her. For decades Montreux has owed fifty percent of its tax revenues to her. The famous hypnotist Fourati had hypnotized her twenty years ago and had been unable to bring her out of the hypnosis. In this way Fourati, as is well known, had ruined not only the lady's life but his own as well.

At the end of the winter a Salzburg couple, who had always worked separately and were now enjoying a joint double pension, hit upon the idea of taking a trip to Zell-on-the-Lake in the Pinzgau, and for this purpose they obtained a brochure on this highly acclaimed town so that they could glance through it to find a small hotel that might suit their purpose for two or three weeks. The couple, who were fond of traveling, did find a hotel in the brochure that seemed to be what they had in mind and seemed to meet their requirements, and they set out on their journey to Zell-on-the-Lake. When, however, they entered the hotel they had chosen, they were forced to the realization that everything they had expected in the hotel was exactly the contrary of their expectations. For example, the rooms described in the brochure as very pleasant were dark, and it seemed to the horrified couple as if a closed coffin had been set down on the floor of every one of those rooms, always with their own name inscribed upon it.

The mayors of Pisa and Venice had agreed to scandalize visitors to their cities, who had for centuries been equally charmed by Venice and Pisa, by secretly and overnight having the tower of Pisa moved to Venice and the campanile of Venice moved to Pisa and set up there. They could not, however, keep their plan a secret, and on the very night on which they were going to have the tower of Pisa moved to Venice and the campanile of Venice moved to Pisa they were committed to the lunatic asylum, the mayor of Pisa in the nature of things to the lunatic asylum in Venice and the mayor of Venice to the lunatic asylum in Pisa. The Italian authorities were able to handle the affair in complete confidentiality.

In June of last year, a Tyrolean was arraigned on a charge of murdering a schoolchild from Imst and was sentenced to life imprisonment. The Tyrolean, a typesetter by profession and employed for thirty years, to the complete satisfaction of the proprietor, in a printing plant in Innsbruck, had attempted to justify his action by testifying that he had been frightened of the schoolchild from Imst, but the jury did not believe him, for the typesetter, who was actually born in Schwaz and whose father had earned great respect as the master of the Tyrolean guild of butchers, was six foot two tall and, as the jury determined in the courtroom, was capable of lifting a three-hundred-pound ball six feet off the ground without faltering. The Tyrolean had murdered the schoolchild from Imst with a so-called *mason's mallet.*

Our uncle, who owned a tobacco factory in Innsbruck and a so-called summer house in Stams and whom, for this reason, we called our Innsbruck uncle, had, on New Year's Day 1967, asked at the main station in Innsbruck for a *round-trip ticket to Merano* and, as we were told by witnesses, had actually boarded a train bound for Merano with an unusually large amount of luggage. He never arrived in Merano, however, and no one has ever heard anything more of him, although the investigation was abandoned only after two years' intensive search. Meanwhile, the tobacco factory, has been closed and the summer house sold because the investigation has consumed all the so-called *fortune* that our Innsbruck uncle had left behind. No buyer has yet been found for the tobacco factory, in which three hundred workers had been employed, who, in the meantime, have all had to be dismissed because the demand for tobacco has fallen in recent years and our uncle's factory is, in fact, out-of-date. We are told, however, that it must be sold if the lawyers who involved themselves in the search for my uncle demand their customary high fees. Each spring we think of how we used to go to Innsbruck and spend the night with our uncle and then go with him next day, at the crack of dawn, to Stams to spend several days in his summer house, reading and going for walks in the surrounding forests. We are convinced that the good health we have enjoyed for so many years is to be attributed first and foremost to the fact that we went to see our uncle, in Innsbruck and in Stams, twice a year, in spring and in autumn. To the accident that our uncle met with on the journey to Merano we attribute the fact that when we now go on a trip, we never buy a *round-trip* ticket, but always ask for a *one-way*.

Firemen from Krems were arraigned because they pulled away the safety blanket they had been holding out and ran away at the very moment at which the suicide, who had for several hours been standing on a ledge on the fifth floor of a Krems apartment building and had threatened to jump to his death, actually jumped. The youngest of the firemen stated in court that he had acted *out of a sudden inner compulsion* and that he had run away, without letting go of the safety blanket, when he saw that the suicide had carried out his threat. As he was the strongest of all the six firemen, he had dragged the other five, together with the safety blanket, along with him, and, at the very moment when the suicide, an unhappy student according to the newspaper, had smashed onto the square in front of the house to which he had been clinging for so long, they had all, he went on to say, flung themselves to the ground and sustained more or less painful injuries. The court before which the fireman who had been the first to run away and who, as we said, being the youngest and the strongest of them, was arraigned as the chief defendant could not deny the responsibility of the chief defendant and acquitted him together with the other five Krems firemen although, in the nature of things, not convinced of his innocence. The Krems fire department has for decades been reputed to be the very best fire department in the world.

So-called speleologists who have made it their life's work to study caves and always attract the greatest interest, especially among those who read the big-city magazines, recently explored the cave between Taxenbach and Schwarzach, which, as we learned from the newspaper, had until then been totally unexplored. At the end of August and in ideal weather conditions, as the *Salzburger Volksblatt* reports, speleologists entered the cave with the firm intention of coming out of the cave again in mid-September. When, however, the speleologists had not come out of the cave even by the end of September, a rescue team had formed, calling itself *The Speleological Rescue Team*, and had set off for the cave to come to the aid of the speleologists who had originally entered the cave at the end of August. But this Speleological Rescue Team itself had not come out of the cave by mid-October, which induced the Salzburg Provincial Government to send a second Speleological Rescue Team into the cave. This second Speleological Rescue Team was composed of the strongest and bravest men in the province and was equipped with the most up-to-date so-called *Cave Rescue Apparatus*. This second Speleological Rescue Team, however, just like the first, entered the cave according to plan but even by the beginning of December had not returned from the cave. At this point the department of the Salzburg Provincial Government responsible for speleology commissioned a firm of building contractors in the Pongau to wall up the cave between Taxenbach and Schwarzach, and this was done before the New Year.

In Lima, a man was arrested who stubbornly maintained that he wished to go into the Andes to look for his wife, who had gone into the Tauern mountains the year before and who, as the man is said to have deposed before the Lima police, had apparently lost her way in the neighborhood of the Tappenkar and fallen into a crevasse. But since the Tauern and, in the nature of things, the Tappenkar too lie in the Salzburg Alps, as even the police officers in Lima knew, it is not surprising that the Peruvian police officers asked the man, whom, in a state of total neglect, wearing only a pair of ragged trousers and a so-called Carinthian peasant shirt, they had arrested in downtown Lima because he had appeared suspicious to them, what he was really after in Peru. The man who was arrested was actually born in Ferlach in Carinthia and was a wealthy Austrian who ran a flourishing gunsmith's business in that town. Our newspaper gave no further details.

On our last trip to the Mölltal, where, no matter what time of year it is, we have always enjoyed ourselves, we were in a tavern in Obervellach that had been recommended to us by a doctor from Linz and had not disappointed us and were chatting with a group of journeyman masons who had gathered at the tavern after work and were playing the zither and singing, thus reminding us once again of the inexhaustible treasures of Carinthian folk music. Late in the evening, the group of journeyman masons came and sat down at our table, and each one of them related something *memorable* or *remarkable* from his own life. We were particularly struck by the journeyman mason who reported that at the age of seventeen, in order to win a bet he had made with a fellow worker, he had climbed the church steeple in Tamsbach, which, as is well known, is very tall. I *almost* fell to my death, said the journeyman mason, and he expressly emphasized that because of this he had *almost* appeared in the newspaper.

The courtroom correspondent is the closest of all to human misery and its absurdity and, in the nature of things, can endure the experience only for a short time, and certainly not for his whole life, without going crazy. The probable, the improbable, even the unbelievable, the most unbelievable are paraded before him every day in the courtroom, and because he has to earn his daily bread by reporting on actual or alleged but in any case, in the nature of things, shameful crimes, he is soon no longer surprised by anything at all. I will, however, tell you about a single incident that still seems to me the most remarkable event of my whole career as a courtroom correspondent. Ferrari, a judge on the Provincial Court of Appeals in Salzburg, for years the dominant figure in the Salzburg Provincial Court—from which, as I said, I reported on everything conceivable—after pronouncing a sentence of twelve years' imprisonment and a fine of eight million schillings on, as he put it in his summation, a vile blackmailer, who was—I remember exactly—a beef exporter from Murau, stood up again and said that he would now set an example. After this unusual announcement, he put his hand under his gown and into his coat pocket as quick as lightning, pulled out a pistol on which the safety catch had already been released, and shot himself—to the horror of all those present in the courtroom—in the left temple. He died instantly.

An old lady who lived near us had gone too far in her charity. She had, as she thought, taken in a *poor Turk*, who at the outset was grateful that he no longer had to live in a hovel scheduled to be torn down but was now—through the charity of the old lady—allowed to live in her town house surrounded by a large garden. He had made himself useful to the old lady as a gardener and, as time went by, was not only completely re-outfitted with clothes by her but was actually pampered by her. One day the Turk appeared at the police station and reported that he had murdered the old lady who had, out of charity, taken him into her house. *Strangled*, as the officers of the court determined on the visit they immediately made to the scene of the crime. When the Turk was asked by the officers of the court why he had murdered the old lady by strangling her, he replied, *out of charity*.

An excursionist who had attached himself to us en route to the so-called Giant World of Ice near Werfen because he was probably of the opinion that we were more entertaining than the other people in our train, which was making its way along the valley, told us he was deeply unhappy over the fact that he had advised one of his colleagues, a bank employee like himself, who had asked him where he should spend his vacation so as to get some relaxation, to take a cruise on the Adriatic and the Mediterranean, something he himself on one occasion had much benefited from. The very ship on which his colleague was bound for Dubrovnik, Corfu, and Alexandria had sunk—for reasons that are still unknown to this day—in the vicinity of Crete, and along with all the others who had gone on this "disaster cruise," as the excursionist called it, his colleague had drowned. He had probably gone down with the ship, which had sunk very rapidly. The loss of the ship and the death of his colleague by drowning had affected him so deeply that for years now he had been unable to find peace. He asked us what he should do to be freed from his guilty conscience, but we dared not give him any advice.

On one occasion as we were approaching Großgmain, where we often used to go with our parents on the weekends, in a so-called landau that dated from the last century and had been built in a workshop in Elixhausen famous for the building of landaus, we saw, in the middle of the forest, a man of about forty or forty-five who tried to stop us as we were traveling fairly fast downhill so as not to be late for our visit to an uncle who was very ill and was living in the hunting lodge that our grandfather had bought from a Prince Liechtenstein at the turn of the century and that he had enlarged for, as he always put it, his *philosophical purposes*; the man had placed himself in the middle of the road and had had the audacity to grab at the horses' harness in order to force our landau to stop—which, naturally, he did not succeed in doing. The man had in fact only managed to jump aside at the last moment and, as I could indistinctly ascertain in the gathering darkness, escape after turning several somersaults. The fact was, we thought we had come upon one of those characters who do their mischief here along the Austro-Bavarian frontier and who had escaped from one of our numerous penal establishments—as legalese will have it—which was another reason for our not stopping. In fact, we would even have run over this stranger who suddenly popped up in front of us, to avoid, as we thought, becoming the victims of a crime. The following day, a forest worker who was employed by my uncle called our attention to the fact that a man had been found frozen to death, after sustaining severe injuries, in the forest through which we had traveled in our landau the previous evening—a man who was, as it transpired, the best workman and the most loyal man that my uncle had ever had. In the nature of things, we did not breathe a word about our adventure of the previous evening, and we expressed our sympathy for the widow of the man who had met such a tragic end.

SUSPICION

A Frenchman was arrested in the notorious town of Kitzbühel solely on the grounds that a chambermaid in the Double Eagle Hotel had accused him of trying to molest her when she had come, at his request, to serve him a triple cognac in his room around midnight; this the Frenchman, according to reports in the newspaper, categorically denied, calling it a *base and malicious Alpine calumny*. The Frenchman was a professor of German at the famous Paris Sorbonne and had intended to recover, in the Double Eagle Hotel in Kitzbühel, from the strain of completing a translation of Nietzsche's *Thus Spake Zarathustra* that he had undertaken, which had occupied him for more than two years. However, the abrupt change from the climate of Paris to the climate of Kitzbühel had, in the nature of things, not been good for him, and the result of his hurried journey from France to the Tyrol had been a very bad case of the flu, which he had contracted immediately after his arrival in Kitzbühel and which had forced him to stay in bed for several days. As it was taken as proven that the French professor lacked all the preconditions for seducing the chambermaid, let alone for actually violating her, he was released from custody after a few hours, and he returned to the Double Eagle. The chambermaid was driven out of the Double Eagle, and when she discovered her picture in the newspaper with the caption *A Disgraceful Kitzbühel Woman*, she immediately drowned herself in the Inn River. The body has not been found to this day.

The thinker of whom it was said that he thought day and night and even in his sleep arrived in Vöcklabruck one day and, after making inquiries in the main square about a high-class inn, went to the Capercaillie, which is highly regarded by everyone and in which, it is said, the cuisine is the most reliable in Austria. Even the thinker was not disappointed in the Capercaillie; on the contrary, the food and drink were far better than he had expected, and he could not refrain from asking the landlord to come to his table for the one purpose of complimenting him. After the thinker had praised the landlord in terms more glowing than he had ever used to praise anyone in his whole life, he hit upon the idea that in the future it might be better to live not as a thinker but as an innkeeper, and all at once he suggested to the Capercaillie innkeeper that he might like to change places with him. The thinker barely had the words out of his mouth before the Capercaillie innkeeper agreed to the exchange. The Capercaillie innkeeper left the Capercaillie as though he were the thinker and the thinker remained in the Capercaillie as though he were the innkeeper. In the nature of things, neither the innkeeper nor the thinker functioned from that moment on.

Sitting in the early train, we happen to look out of the window just at the moment when we are passing the ravine into which our school group, with whom we had undertaken an excursion to the waterfall, had plunged fifteen years ago, and we think about how we were saved but the others were killed forever. The teacher who had been taking our group to the waterfall hanged herself immediately after a sentence of eight years' imprisonment had been passed on her by the Salzburg Provincial Court. When the train passes the scene of the accident, we can hear our own cries intermingled with the cries of the whole group.

On the Großglockner after a climb of several hours, two professors, close friends, from the University of Göttingen, who had been staying in Heiligenstadt, had reached the spot in front of the telescope which is mounted above the glacier. Skeptics though they were, they could not fail to be impressed by the unique beauty of the mountains, as they had constantly assured one another, and when they arrived at the spot where the telescope was mounted, one of them kept asking the other to be the first to look through the telescope, so as to avoid being reproached by the other for pushing himself forward in order to look through the telescope first. Finally they agreed that the older and more cultivated and, in the nature of things, the more courteous should take the first look through the telescope, and he was overcome by what he saw. However, when his colleague approached the telescope, he had hardly put his eye to it when he gave a shrill cry and dropped dead. To this day, the friend of the man who died in this remarkable way still wonders, in the nature of things, what his colleague *actually* saw in the telescope, for he certainly did not see *the same thing*.

Even though I have always hated zoological gardens and actually find that my suspicions are aroused by people who visit zoological gardens, I still could not avoid going out to Schönbrunn on one occasion and, at the request of my companion, a professor of theology, standing in front of the monkeys' cage to look at the monkeys, which my companion fed with some food he had brought with him for the purpose. The professor of theology, an old friend of mine from the university, who had asked me to go to Schönbrunn with him had, as time went on, fed all the food he had brought with him to the monkeys, when suddenly the monkeys, for their part, scratched together all the food that had fallen to the ground and offered it to us through the bars. The professor of theology and I were so startled by the monkeys' sudden behavior that in a flash we turned on our heels and left Schönbrunn through the nearest exit.

We had no luck with the weather and the guests at our table were repellent in every respect. They even spoiled Nietzsche for us. Even after they had had a fatal car accident and had been laid out in the church in Sils, we still hated them.

In the immediate neighborhood of Aurach, after we had climbed the
Hongar and then, beginning the descent, had walked along the ridge
towards the Höllengebirge for five hours, we visited Haumer, the log-
ger, of whom we had heard nothing for a long time. Haumer did not
open his door to us even after we had knocked repeatedly, although we
were sure our assumption that he was at home was correct. When
we had already left his house, we suddenly had the impression he had
now heard us and wanted to open up for us, and we went back to his
house. Haumer—whom we had known from our earliest childhood
and who had been closer to us than anyone—did, in fact, open the
door and invited us to sit down in the so-called downstairs parlor. It
was only after we had been sitting on the benches in the downstairs
parlor for a while that we realized that Haumer had still not said a
word to us. We stayed more than an hour with him and then we took
our leave without his having uttered a single word. It was not until the
next day, while talking to my cousin about the meeting, that I learned
that Haumer had lost his hearing and his speech more than four years
before as the result of a gun salute that he himself had fired on his
daughter's wedding-day when she married a butcher's apprentice
from Nussdorf. At the same time it became clear to me that it was over
four years since I had visited Haumer, the very person, I thought, to
whom I owe so much.

A comic actor who had for decades earned his living by being funny and who had always filled every hall in which he appeared to the very last seat suddenly became the long-expected sensation for a group of Bavarian excursionists who had come across him on the rocky ledge above the so-called Salzburg horse-pond. The actor stated, in front of the group of excursionists, that just as he was, in his lederhosen and with his Tyrolean hat on his head, he would throw himself off the ledge, at which the group of excursionists had as usual burst into loud laughter. But the actor is reported to have said that he was in earnest and to have immediately thrown himself off.

A paterfamilias who had for decades been praised and beloved for a so-called *extraordinary sense of family* and who one Saturday afternoon, admittedly in especially humid weather, murdered four of his six children, defended himself in court by saying that all of a sudden the children were *too much* for him.

Last week in Linz 180 people died who had the flu that is currently raging in Linz, but they died not from the flu but as the result of a prescription that was misunderstood by a newly appointed pharmacist. The pharmacist will probably be charged with reckless homicide, possibly, according to the paper, *even before Christmas.*

Several Englishmen who were inveigled by a mountain guide in eastern Tyrol into climbing the Drei Zinnen with him were so disappointed, after reaching the highest of the three peaks, with what Nature had to offer them on this highest peak that then and there they killed the guide, a family man with three children and, it seems, a deaf wife. When, however, they realized what they had actually done, they threw themselves off the peak, one after the other. After this, a newspaper in Birmingham wrote that Birmingham had lost its most outstanding newspaper publisher, its most extraordinary bank director, and its most able undertaker.

A so-called *Chamber Music Association* famous for playing only ancient music on original instruments and for having only Rossini, Frescobaldi, Vivaldi, and Pergolesi in its repertoire was playing in an old castle on the Attersee and had its greatest success since it was founded. The applause continued until the Chamber Music Association did not have a single encore left on its program to play. It was not until the next day that the musicians were told that they had been playing in an institute for deaf-mutes.

A hairdresser who suddenly went mad and decapitated a duke, allegedly a member of the royal family, with a razor and who is now in the lunatic asylum in Reading—formerly the famous Reading Jail—is said to have declared himself ready to make his head available for those scientific purposes which, in his opinion, would be rewarded with the Nobel Prize within at least eight or ten years.

On his way back from Moscow, where he had been the guest of the Academy of Sciences, the world-famous French philosopher who has for decades been called the most important of his time came to Vienna to give the same lecture to the Viennese Academy of Sciences that he had already given in Moscow. After his lecture I was the guest of two professors and members of the Viennese Academy who, like me, had heard the French philosopher's lecture. The one called the lecture, and thus the French philosopher as well, profound, the other called it shallow, and both of them produced solid grounds for their assertions.

In Vienna we had invited a so-called *scholar* to dinner with the object of his bringing us up to date on current trends in the intellectual and artistic worlds, something in which we had always taken the liveliest interest. However, instead of granting our wish to acquire a greater knowledge of philosophy, literature, and art, the scholar, a recognized professor at the University of Vienna, used our invitation for the sole purpose of enlightening us about what, in his opinion, was the bad character of that colleague of his who had recently published a book on the very subject that is the subject of our visitor's lifelong study. The following day our guest was at the home of one of our friends who is a friend of the professor whom our guest had belittled in front of us in the coarsest manner the day before, and there he accorded his rival first place, ahead of all the others, not only as to his character but as to his scholarship as well.

Professor Moosprugger said that he had gone to the West station in Vienna to pick up a colleague whom he did not know personally but knew only from correspondence. He had expected a different person from the one who actually arrived at the West station. When I drew Moosprugger's attention to the fact that the person who arrives is always someone different from the person we expect, he got up and left simply and solely for the purpose of breaking off and abandoning all the contacts he had ever established throughout his life.

For years after our mother's death, the post office continued to deliver letters that were addressed to her. The post office had taken no notice of her death.

A man from Augsburg was committed to the Augsburg lunatic asylum merely because, throughout his life, he had claimed at every possible opportunity that Goethe's last words were *mehr nicht* (no more) rather than *mehr Licht* (more light), something that, in the long run and as time went on, is said to have so frayed the nerves of those with whom he came in contact that they banded together to get this Augsburger, so unhappily obsessed with his claim, committed to a lunatic asylum. It is reported that six doctors refused to commit him to a lunatic asylum but that the seventh immediately arranged to have him committed. This doctor was, as I learned from the *Frankfurter Allgemeine Zeitung*, decorated with the Goethe badge of the City of Frankfurt for his efforts.

Four actors from a theater company hit upon the idea of writing a comedy themselves after the products of comic playwrights had become more and more odious and boring to them, and all four of them immediately sat down and started to write, in the nature of things, only about themselves, although their original intention had been that *each of them would write a part for himself in the comedy*, for which, after thorough and, in fact, weeks-long study, they could come up with no other title than *The Author*, and twelve weeks after they had hit upon the idea they produced the comedy in their theater. But it is reported that even with this *Author* they had no success.

A businessman from Koblenz had made his life's dream come true by visiting the pyramids of Giza and was forced, after he had done visiting the pyramids, to describe his visit as the greatest disappointment of his life, which I understand, for I myself was in Egypt last year and was disappointed above all by the pyramids. However, whereas I very quickly overcame my disappointment, the Koblenz businessman took vengeance for his disappointment by placing, for months on end, full-page advertisements in all the major newspapers in Germany, Switzerland, and Austria, warning all future visitors to Egypt against the pyramids and especially against the pyramids of Cheops, which had disappointed him most deeply, more than all the others. The Koblenz businessman used up his resources in a very short time with these—as he called them—anti-Egypt and anti-pyramid advertisements and plunged himself into total penury. In the nature of things, his advertisements did not have the influence upon people that he had hoped for; on the contrary, the number of visitors to Egypt this year, as opposed to last year, has doubled.

My former classmate who emigrated to Australia eleven years ago and returned to his Styrian homeland two years ago emigrated to Australia again six months ago, although he knows he will return to Styria again and will continue to emigrate to Australia and return to Styria as often as it takes him to find peace either in Australia or in Styria. His father before him, a journeyman baker from the Mölltal who went to school with my father, emigrated from Carinthia to Styria at least twenty times and each time returned to Carinthia from Styria until he finally found peace in Carinthia, in Arndorf near St. Veit-on-the-Glan, where in the old smithy—his final lodgings—he hanged himself on an iron hook because he was homesick for Styria, without, and he was reproached for this at the time and long after his death, *thinking of his wife and children.*

Because of his acquaintance with a once-gifted composer whom we ourselves for years had dubbed a nonpareil genius, a skilled cabinet-maker from Maria Saal (a favorite place of pilgrimage in Carinthia) discovered literature and wrote poems and little comedies, which, however, according to those who got hold of them, were on the one hand totally *unreadable* and on the other totally *unactable* simply because no one understood them. The cabinetmaker drowned himself in the Längsee on his twenty-second birthday in despair at being so unappreciated. The newspaper that published a short obituary of the unappreciated young man emphasized above all else that he was *unworldly*.

In order to save his wife's life—she had a lung ailment—the man who went by the name of Ofner, the parish man-of-all-work and sexton, bought jointly with his wife, and as our doctor had advised him to, a small piece of wooded land in our neighborhood, high enough up to be out of the mists and in good clean air, and the two of them, after several years' work—supported, of course, by the parish and their immediate neighbors—had built a small house on the property. When, however, the house was finished, Ofner fell ill, because building the house had really been too much for him, and died within a short time. His widow, for whom, after all, the house at the edge of the wood had been intended and who, even after her husband's death, was visibly recovering from her lung ailment, had to get herself a dog, because, of course, now that she was alone, she was afraid. The dog barked at everyone who came within two hundred feet of her house, and as time went by, no one dared to go near it. For years the woman endured being on her own with the dog and without people, when suddenly, in a flash, she could no longer stand the situation and went out and bludgeoned the dog—who had served her so faithfully all the years—to death with a so-called *Sappel*, which loggers use for hauling logs, and threw herself on the mercy of her fellow human beings.

On the Grasberg near Gmunden, a seventy-five-year-old man was found with an Italian passport; he claimed that he came from the village of Reindlmühle at the foot of the Grasberg, which, of course, the police, who had taken him to the Hotel Schachinger in Reindlmühle to warm up—he was suffering from total hypothermia—did not believe. The man, who called himself de Orio in his passport, was, according to his own account, actually called Pfuster and in 1907, when not yet eight years old, had gone with a traveling circus that had set up its big top in Reindlmühle first to Bohemia and from there via Poland and Romania to Italy and had finally stayed with the circus. Shortly before World War II, in 1937 to be precise, he had come back with the circus to Upper Austria and into the Traunsee area, and the circus had, in fact, set up its big top in Reindlmühle again. At that time, however, so he said, he had not revealed his true identity and had not had the slightest desire to stay in Reindlmühle; he had left with the circus again, this time for Hungary and Macedonia. It was only now, when he had, so to speak, reached the end of his tether, that he had made the effort to return to Reindlmühle. After a short time the police established that the man's statements—he actually did come from Reindlmühle though he was officially an Italian—were true. It was also made known that for a long time people had thought the young Pfuster had fallen into the raging river Aurach and had been washed away.

Many years ago a photographer took up residence in Ebensee; from the very first day he was rumored to have spent several years in prison for having molested a thirteen-year-old boy from Ischl. Not a single person had their photograph taken by the photographer, who expected to do good business in Ebensee, where so many weddings take place throughout the year, or at the very least to make a decent income, and he finally had to close down his business and move out again. It is said that there was no truth to the rumor; it was originally spread by the Traunkirchen photographer Strößner. Strößner has now stated that his colleague has committed suicide, but it is not known how.

In Alsace we learned that a man from Selestadt in Colmar had been placed in the old people's home because his family had stated that he was eighty years old, which was borne out by his papers; he himself, however, had constantly maintained that he was only sixty years old, until the family could stand it no longer and determined to hand him over to the old people's home in Colmar. Indeed, the man had reiterated his claim day and night and had, in other ways as well, made his family's life a *horror*. He is said not to have washed for years and to have always walked around barefoot and to have exposed himself, from time to time, totally naked on the street, all of which would have sufficed to have him committed to a lunatic asylum, which they did not want to do to him. And so they determined to send him to Colmar. After reaching Colmar with the greatest difficulty, he had broken away from the nuns who were taking him into the old people's home and could only be recaptured several hours later. The nuns did, however, persuade him to enter the old people's home without putting up any resistance. During the night, the man, whose name is stated to be Schluemberger, set fire to the old people's home in Colmar, and all 478 inmates were burned to death. And so was he.

At the foot of the Ortles, a Turin industrialist had a world-famous architect build a hotel for his twenty-two-year-old son which on its completion was described as the most modern and expensive hotel, and not only in the whole of Italy; it was twelve stories high and actually took only eighteen months to build. Before work was begun on the building, a road nineteen kilometers long had to be constructed into what was, until then, completely inaccessible countryside, some of the most unspoiled in the whole of the Alps, which the industrialist from Turin had first noticed on a walking tour he had undertaken with some English friends and which had at once seemed suitable for the building of such a hotel. About one thousand workers are said to have found work on the site. On the day before the hotel was to be opened, the son of the ambitious native of Turin had a fatal accident on the automobile race track in Monza. As a result, the opening ceremonies at the hotel did not take place. The unhappy father decided, on the day of his son's funeral, never again to set foot in the just-completed hotel and to let it fall into total disrepair from that day on. He paid off and dismissed all the people who had already been engaged as necessary for running the hotel, blocked off the approach road, and forbade anyone to enter the valley at the end of which the hotel stands. We came upon the hotel after leaving Gomagoi while on a walking tour in the Ortles Mountains, three years after its completion; even at that time it made a shocking impression on us. Years of storms had long since destroyed the windows and had taken off large parts of the roofs, and tall trees, probably pines, were already growing out of the still fully equipped kitchen.

MIMOSA

A friend of our mother's, on her way to Herzegovina, whence she had intended to repair to Montenegro for several weeks, stopped off in Cavtat and, while there, visited the cemetery famous both for its unique location across from Dubrovnik and for the Mestrovic mausoleum there. Across from the mausoleum, as she told us, she suddenly discovered a tombstone bearing the name of Tino Pattiera, a favorite of hers who was once the most celebrated singer in the Vienna Opera, and it occurred to her at that moment that her favorite singer came from Cavtat, which was once called Ragusaveggia. She had not known that the singer Pattiera was dead. In her distress, she went down to Cavtat, which is also famous for its mimosa, and returned to the cemetery with a bunch of mimosa to lay on Pattiera's grave. In the nature of things, her trip to Montenegro was overshadowed by her experience in Cavtat. Her astonishment must have been beyond bounds when, after returning to Vienna, she read the announcement that Pattiera would be singing next day in *Tosca*, her favorite opera. And, in fact, Pattiera did sing in this *Tosca* as the announcement had stated, and our mother's friend managed to convince herself in the opera—which was sold out—of the singer's still brilliant voice: there was no way she could have known that Pattiera had bought himself a burial plot in his native Cavtat while he was still alive and had had his name chiseled on the white marble stone that had misled our mother's friend, who had been an opera enthusiast all her life.

In Maloja we made the acquaintance of a once-famous male dancer in the Paris Opera, who was brought in a wheelchair into our hotel one evening by a young Italian from Castasegna whom the dancer had engaged for a period of several years. As we learned from the dancer, he had collapsed in mid-performance on the first night of Handel's *Raphael*, which had been specially choreographed for him by Béjart, and he had been paralyzed ever since. The dancer said he had suddenly lost consciousness and only two days later had come to. It was possible, according to the dancer, who was wrapped in very expensive nutria fur, that his misfortune could be traced back to the fact that for the first time in his career he had thought about the complexity of a combination of steps that he had been afraid of for the whole fifteen years of his career and that had taken him to all the great opera houses of the world. A dancer, in his opinion, ought never to think about his dance while he is dancing; he should only dance, nothing else.

Twenty years ago at the Actors' Club in Warsaw, where the best conversation was to be had and the best food was to be found, I met the wife of a so-called surrealist painter well known in Poland; she has, among other things, translated Thomas Mann's *Magic Mountain* into Polish and is one of the most cultured women in Poland. It was only at the end of our conversation that she mentioned what a terrible situation she was in—her husband was lying at death's door in a Warsaw hospital and she had come out that evening for the first time in a year to be among people. I had the pleasure of meeting her on several occasions and of having conversations with her about German and Polish literature and art. And, of course, I also discussed politics with her and repeatedly expressed my admiration for the Poles. When back in Warsaw ten years later, I naturally called on her. But she greeted me at the door with the announcement that her husband was at death's door, which led me to think she was mad. But in fact she had been remarried for almost ten years after the death of her first husband, and now her second husband was in the same hospital as her first and with the same illness, which she did not tell me at once. Naturally I invited her to the Actors' Club, and once again she told me that she had not been out for a year and of course not to the Actors' Club. When I went back to Warsaw after another ten years, I did not visit her, though I missed her all the time I was there and, in the nature of things, had a guilty conscience.

The most interesting foreigners always put up at the Warsaw Hotel Saski, where I have stayed on several occasions, and it is for this reason that I always go to the Hotel *Saski* and not the *Bristol* or the *Europejski*, which have always disappointed me. One evening, close to midnight, when I was sitting all alone in the lower lobby, a gentleman sat down at my table and told me the following story. He said he had left the hotel about two hours before to catch a bus to Wilanow, where he had an appointment with a business partner in the vicinity of the Royal Palace; he hated taxis, he said, and it was for this reason, and not because it was cheaper, that he always traveled by bus. Polish buses, he took this opportunity of telling me, were the most comfortable in the whole world, and no matter how many people were crammed into them the air was always of the best quality. In any case, he loved Poland more than any other country, which I can understand, for I know of no country that I like better. He was born in Silesia but held a Canadian passport and probably was always accustomed to talking alternately in German and English, a manner of speaking that I have always found attractive and stimulating. On that evening, however, when the stranger, according to his custom, left the Hotel Saski and went to the bus stop, he suddenly had no idea *what* he was doing out in the street and went back into the Hotel Saski again. But as he had no idea *why* he had left the hotel and gone to the bus stop, he could not settle down in the Hotel Saski and left the Hotel Saski again and spent two hours walking around the Hotel Saski. About ten minutes ago, he said, he suddenly remembered that he had wanted to go to Wilanow to meet the above-mentioned business partner. But by then it was too late to go out to Wilanow and he decided to go back into the hotel, sit down in the lobby, and drink a glass of whisky. He was still very upset by the incident and ordered two glasses of whisky, one for himself and one for me.

PICCADILLY CIRCUS

A colleague of my cousin's who had recently been in London told him that during his stay in London he was suddenly seized—between ten and eleven o'clock at night in Piccadilly Circus—with the idea of boarding an Underground train, no matter what line, and traveling to the end of the line as he had often done before, because for as long as he could remember there was nothing in the world about which he was so enthusiastic as the London Underground, which could not be compared with any other underground railway in the whole world and certainly not with the Paris Métro, which had so disappointed him the first time he had traveled on it that he had decided never to set foot in the city of Paris again. My cousin's colleague would scarcely arrive in London before he would take some Underground train or other and travel on it for as long as he could, and, in fact, he had traveled so often on all the Underground lines in London that he had lost count of how often. In fact, on the day in question he had traveled on the Underground several times, but even by ten in the evening he had still not had enough of it. But then, as the Underground enthusiast said to my cousin, when the Underground train entered the station and the automatic doors opened, the passengers who were jammed up against the door fell out of the train totally rigid and dead, and the others remained, equally rigid and dead, standing or sitting in the train. Shocked as he was—he was the only person waiting on the platform—he ran back up to Piccadilly Circus. He claims, however, that when he told the Underground officials of his experience, they merely shook their heads. He then went to Knightsbridge to recover. Since that time, he says, he has never traveled on the Underground.

A woman with forty-eight previous convictions, described by the presiding judge of the district court in Wels, right at the opening of her *by then most recent trial*—the Wels paper reports—as *a thieving old woman well known to the court*, was on this occasion accused of stealing a pair of, for her, completely useless opera glasses from a recently deceased female opera-goer who had, however, been completely unable to walk for many years and was no longer able to go to the opera, for which reasons she had long not used the opera glasses and had in fact forgotten that she had them—all of which came out in the course of the proceedings. The woman was able to increase her original sentence, which was only three months' imprisonment, by six months by means of boxing the judge's ears as soon as sentence was passed. She said she had hoped to get at least nine months in prison because she could not stand being free any longer.

In the *Zur Wies* inn, where we often get together with the woodsmen when we want to be enlightened about their problems and also to be better entertained than anywhere else, a man turned up just before Christmas 1953 who immediately attracted our attention by his taciturnity. It was immediately clear to us that the man, whom we had never seen before, must be of peasant stock, because he did not take his hat off when he sat down in the bar. It was not clear what the man, who was about thirty, was after; he was not visiting relatives in the area, he seemed too poorly dressed for that; his clothes were worn and even ragged in places. Once our curiosity was aroused, we asked him to come and sit at our table and to join in our conversation, and he came and sat with us and we ordered him a beer. It was already quite late when the man said he was looking for a wife and asked us whether we knew of one that would suit him and where he could find her. Relaxed as we were, we played a joke on him, sending him, close to midnight, into the so-called Frauengraben, a gorge with a small but sometimes torrential stream running through it, a place never reached by the sunshine. A woman of about fifty lived in the Frauengraben; her arms and legs and, indeed, her whole body were deformed, but she was highly thought of for her total love of animals and her goodness of heart. The man did not come out of the Frauengraben again for ten years, and when he did come out after those ten years it was for the sole purpose of marrying the deformed woman in the little church in Reindlmühle. After their wedding, the couple disappeared into the Frauengraben for another ten years. They are said to be happy.

Polish animal tamers are famous for not making mistakes. Now, however, a case has come to light in which a Polish animal tamer did make a mistake. The animal tamer, Lutoslawsky, who was formerly to be seen with the Krone Circus and the Sarassani Circus, had, after performing his famous panther number in his native city of Cracow, invited the mayor of Cracow, who was seated in the front row, to perform the panther number as he had done, the high point of the number being that the most agile of the panthers had to jump through a burning hoop. Until then, Lutoslawsky had been used to having everyone he asked to perform this suicidal trick refuse, in the nature of things, to do it, whereupon the panther number was finished and the next, the number with the talking donkey, began. The mayor of Cracow, however, to everyone's surprise and to the animal tamer's horror, accepted the challenge and entered the panthers' cage, asked for and received the animal tamer's whip, and, while Lutoslawsky watched the scene with his back to the bars of the cage, performed exactly the same number with the panthers that Lutoslawsky had done. It seemed to the audience that in the hands of the mayor of Cracow the number was much more exciting and even more artistic than in the hands of Lutoslawsky, and so, as is always said of enthusiasm, they *heaped applause* upon their mayor, whereas they had booed Lutoslawsky. Suddenly, in the midst of the applause, the panthers, which until then had been sitting quietly upon their stools, flung themselves onto Lutoslawsky and tore him limb from limb before the eyes of the horrified audience. Why they didn't fling themselves onto the mayor, who managed to escape to safety, completely unharmed by the panthers, is what the Polish newspapers are asking.

In the Belgian city of Bruges a few hundred years ago, a nine-year-old chorister who had sung a wrong note in a mass that was being performed before the entire royal court in the Bruges cathedral is said to have been beheaded. It seems that the queen had fainted as a result of the wrong note sung by the chorister and had remained unconscious until her death. The king is supposed to have sworn an oath that, if the queen did not come round, he would have not only the guilty chorister but all the choristers in Bruges beheaded, which he did after the queen had not come to and had died. For centuries no sung masses were to be heard in Bruges.

A so-called *Auszügler*, a former farmer who had already turned over his farm to his son and had been living on his own for eleven years on the ground floor in what had formerly been a cellar, was found dead by the postman, who was attempting to deliver his pension, in Breitenschützing, an Upper Austrian village which, because of the heavy fog that enshrouds it almost all autumn and all winter long, has driven many of the inhabitants of Breitenschützing mad. The *Auszügler*, an invalid who had lost his right leg in World War II in the Caucasus and had received the Iron Cross Class One for bravery in the face of the enemy, had, so as not to freeze to death and because his son and daughter-in-law, who were always fighting, had ignored their father and father-in-law for months and not given him any wood, finally thrown his wooden leg into the open fireplace, as the police discovered in their investigation, but in spite of this he froze to death when the fire burned out. The son and the daughter-in-law have both been reported to the police.

Last week we witnessed the spectacle of five cows running, one after the other, into the express train in which we had to return to Vienna and of seeing them cut all to pieces. After the track had been cleared by the train crew and even by the driver, who came along with a pick-ax, the train proceeded after a delay of about forty minutes. Looking out of the window I caught sight of the milkmaid as she ran screaming towards a farmyard in the dusk.

The fortune-teller Gruber, in Wels, was murdered by the haulage contractor to whom he had prophesied that his wife would die before the year was out. Under the pretext of showing him the house he had built for himself, the haulage contractor had lured Gruber into his future dwelling in Lichtenau, killed him, and walled him up in a so-called blind passage in the cellar. In court, the haulage contractor admitted that as early as March he had decided to murder Gruber, the fortune-teller, if his wife lived past Christmas. Between Boxing Day and New Year's Eve he arranged a time for Gruber to come and visit him to drink to the New Year and to see how he had realized his ideas in his new house. Gruber is described as unsuspecting, the haulage contractor as crafty. The famous Viennese specialist in forensic medicine, Breitenegger, was able to determine the time of Gruber's death to the minute, even after eight weeks. The haulage contractor had been carrying on an affair with a Leonding needle-woman for years.

A loden coat that was washed up by the River Traun near Steirermühl has again not succeeded in clearing up the mystery of an accident that occurred two and a half years ago. The loden coat has been indisputably identified as the loden coat belonging to Irrsiegler, the cement worker. To this day Irrsiegler has been desperately sought by his family because he is the only person who knows where, at the end of the war in 1945, his father buried the fortune in gold coins on which the family had pinned its hopes but which Irrsiegler had not intended to dig up until New Year's Day 1974 because his father had extracted a promise from him not to dig up the treasure, the actual origin of which is unknown, until New Year's Day 1974. Irrsiegler was found dead immediately below the place where his loden coat was washed up. He must have been in the water for several weeks. Where he had spent the rest of the time, a period of almost two and a half years, is unknown. At the time of his disappearance Irrsiegler had gone to the Gasthaus Anschütz to get a beer and had not returned.

The papermaker Filzmoser shot his neighbor Nöstlinger, who, like him, was employed in the paper mill in Steirermühl, *by mistake*, as he stated in court. He had shot at a pheasant that suddenly flew up out of the undergrowth in the so-called Peiskamer Forest, but instead of hitting the pheasant he had hit Nöstlinger, with whom he had regularly gone hunting for twenty-five years. Nöstlinger died immediately. He stated that he, Filzmoser, and Nöstlinger had been lifelong friends. Witnesses testified in court that the two men had not spoken to each other since the moment when Nöstlinger had obtained a loan to build an extension to his house and had been able to start building the extension at once. The reason was that Filzmoser had been denied a similar loan by the same place in Linz. It is well known that in the area of the River Traun a lot of men obtain a hunting permit solely for the purpose of committing murder.

The husband returned alone, after about four hours, from a boat
trip that the couple had taken one evening from Traunkirchen to
Rindbach; on the Tuesday evening at about nine o'clock he arrived at
the fisherman Moser's in a state of great agitation and stated that
during the storm that had suddenly arisen his wife had been thrown
out of the boat, one of the old skiffs that are still to be found on the
Traun lake, and had drowned. He had done all in his power to save her.
His wife had suddenly gone down. Finally, he stated, he had feared for
his own life and had turned back and had managed with the greatest
difficulty to reach the shore. A search undertaken on the following
day yielded no results. Three days later, after all hope had been abandoned, the husband had held a service in the parish church, and a year
later he installed a black marble tablet to the memory of his drowned
wife in the wall of that same church that was closest to the lake.
Shortly afterwards he got married. That was in 1973. Two years later,
divers discovered a body on the lake bed and, as the weather was favorable, brought it up onto the shore; the body had a cord around its
neck, and attached to the cord was a boundary stone from Altmünster
parish. The body was that of the woman alleged to have drowned.

The lives of two brothers had developed in a way that in the nature of things was appropriate to their dispositions, and they had gone their opposite ways and had, in the course of time, grown completely apart from one another. We liked both of them and had, in fact, for decades carefully observed their capabilities, those of the philosophical one and those of the one who was in business, and we were alternately attracted by these capabilities and repelled by them, at times more by the philosophical capabilities of the one brother, at others by the commercial ones of the other. When we were all over thirty, we suddenly could no longer count on our relationships being restored to their old intimacy, and we lost sight of the two brothers. Eventually, however, we learned of the importance and the fame of our former friends and of the circumstance that it was precisely this importance and fame that had driven them apart and, as time went by, totally isolated them. The one brother now lived for nothing but his philosophy, the other only for his business dealings. When one of them died, his relatives said he had *worked himself to death*. A year later, when the other one died, they said he had *read himself to death*. At the crucial point in their lives, each had gone his own separate and, of necessity, opposite, way to his death.

At the funeral of a woodcutter from Irresberg, with whom we had been having a drink in the tavern just three days before and from whom we had learned so much more about the countryside and the people immediately around us than we had from anybody else, we were, in the nature of things, more thoughtful than at other funerals. How could it be that more associations and, above all, more complex ones could all at once be brought to light by such a simple person than by others whom we had considered not simple but complex? The woodcutter, who had been known to us for decades and with whom we had been on friendly terms, as we are with almost all the woodcutters in the neighborhood, had throughout these decades scarcely ever expressed himself as openly as he did on what was, for him, his last evening in the tavern; all at once his accounts revealed a different countryside and different people and are now for us the only authentic ones. The man had spent several hours explaining his world and, indeed, *the* world and had, after presenting his explanations to us, fallen silent again at what we thought was the appropriate time for him. On his way home, however, he had fallen into the Aurach and drowned. Some schoolchildren had found him. The principal of the school gave a short speech at his graveside and said that his friend the woodcutter had been a *natural* human being.

In the cemetery in Elixhausen, some workmen who had been hired to build a crypt for the late owner of a cheese factory excavated, at a depth of about two feet, the skeleton of a man who must have been nine feet tall and who had apparently been buried 150 years ago. As far back as anyone can recall, only very short people are thought to have lived in Elixhausen.

It must have been disturbed self-awareness that caused a professor of natural history from Salzburg to box the ears of one of his pupils, for no reason at all, according to the pupil, who had then lost his hearing. The pupil's father, a master plasterer who had visions of sending his son to the Technical University in Vienna and making a famous architect out of him, had an acquaintance who was an officially sworn appraiser calculate the sum his son would have earned by his sixty-fifth birthday if he had pursued in orderly fashion—as the expert witness's testimony states—and successfully attained the career goals his father had intended for him, and he sued the professor of natural history for this amount. The sum of 230,000,000 schillings was the minimum sum that would be accepted and was thus to be recovered, stated the expert witness on the instructions of the father of the son who had been struck deaf and who had leaped into the well-known Liechtenberg gorge three days previously. The proceedings were adjourned. The professor of natural history was suspended for several months because the mistreatment of schoolchildren is forbidden. He testified before the arbitration tribunal charged with his case that he had *forgotten* that corporal punishment had long since been forbidden.

It was significant, said a member of the Provincial Parliament at a session of the Salzburg Provincial Parliament—after that parliament had been discussing the fact that the number of schoolchildren who had killed themselves in Salzburg the previous year by jumping off a ledge on one of the steep hills in the city or by drowning themselves in the River Salzach had doubled since the year before—that the children who commit suicide in Salzburg come from the so-called middle classes. As is well known, Salzburg has the highest suicide rate among schoolchildren in the world. The more highly thought-of the beauty of a city is, according to the member of parliament, the higher the suicide rate, and not, as was previously assumed, the reverse. The question is, he said, how the problem of schoolchildren's suicide in Salzburg, which has become one of its most urgent problems and has already become the subject of international discussion and astonishment, is to be dealt with officially. He, a socialist member, now faces the question, after the fourteen-year-old son of a gardener employed by the city had thrown himself off the so-called Humboldt terrace and had been smashed to pieces, whether this incident is not an indication that the working class has already moved up into the middle class and should possibly for some time have been reckoned part of the bourgeoisie.

In the large reading room of the Salzburg University library, the librarian hanged himself from the large chandelier because, as he wrote in a suicide note, after twenty-two years of service he could no longer bear to reshelve and lend out books that were only written for the sake of wreaking havoc, and this, he said, applied to every book that had ever been written. This reminded me of my grandfather's brother who was the huntsman in charge of the forest district of Altentann near Hennsdorf and who shot himself on the summit of the Zifanken because he could no longer bear human misery. He too left this insight of his in a note.

Pittioni, the geography teacher who was tormented by his pupils the whole time he taught in a secondary school, failed to return from a vacation. He had gone to Hüttschlag just to study the works of Humboldt and to relax, but he hanged himself in the room to which he had retired *for just a few days*. In his will he left everything he was possessed of to his pupils. They should not think he hated them now that he had drawn the only conclusion open to him, he wrote in his will. On the contrary. They had not accepted his love for them, no matter how much he had done for them. Whatever the reason, he hoped for their forgiveness.

In Pontebba, twenty-two years after an avalanche that had destroyed half the town, an entire bus that had been fully occupied at the time of the avalanche was excavated. The passengers were, as the papers report, still well preserved and sitting on their seats, and every one of them had a small blue label around his or her neck with "Destination *Munich*" stamped on it. At the time, as was later established, an exhibition of icons had taken place in Munich at which an icon from Pontebba was displayed.

TRUE LOVE

An Italian who owns a villa in Riva on Lake Garda and can live very comfortably on the interest from the estate his father left him has, according to a report in *La Stampa*, been living for the last twelve years with a mannequin. The inhabitants of Riva report that on mild evenings they have observed the Italian, who is said to have studied art history, boarding a glass-domed deluxe boat, which is moored not far from his home, with the mannequin to take a ride on the lake. Described years ago as incestuous in a reader's letter addressed to the newspaper published in Desencano, he had applied to the appropriate civil authorities for permission to marry his mannequin but was refused. The church too had denied him the right to marry his mannequin. In winter he regularly leaves Lake Garda in mid-December and goes with his beloved, whom he met in a Paris shop-window, to Sicily, where he regularly rents a room in the famous Hotel Timeo in Taormina to escape from the cold, which, all assertions to the contrary, gets unbearable on Lake Garda every year after mid-December.

A playwright whose plays have been performed in all the major theaters made it a matter of principle not to go to any of these productions, and for years, enjoying greater and greater success, he was able to hold fast to this principle. He had resolutely rejected all invitations from theater managements to see their productions, leaving most of their requests unanswered. Besides, there was nothing he hated more than theater managers. One day he broke with his principle and went to the Düsseldorf theater—considered at the time one of the best houses, which, in the nature of things, means that the Düsseldorf theater was in fact one of the best theaters in Germany—and saw his latest play being performed there, not, in the nature of things, on the opening night but at the third or fourth performance. After he had seen what the Düsseldorf players had made of his play, he filed a complaint in the Düsseldorf court that had jurisdiction over such matters, and this was enough to have him committed, before the trial took place, to the famous Bethel lunatic asylum in nearby Bielefeld. He sued the manager of the Düsseldorf theater for the return of his play, which meant nothing short of demanding that everyone involved in his play in any manner whatsoever produce and return anything that had the least connection with his play. Of course he also demanded that the people in the audiences, nearly five thousand of them, who had already seen his play return to him what they had seen.

Another playwright testifying in court—before which he had been summoned by an aggrieved theatergoer who felt himself denigrated by the playwright on the stage of the Bochum theater, which the playwright, even in front of the court, kept referring to as the Bochum lunatic asylum, in which, he stated, there were really no actors but only fools sustained by the director of a lunatic asylum who was merely pretending to be a theater manager, performing throughout the year to an uncomprehending audience—stated that he enjoyed such great success only because, in contrast to his unsuccessful colleagues, he was honest enough to pretend that his comedies were always tragedies and his tragedies comedies. When he had, on one occasion, actually called a tragedy a tragedy, he had suffered a tremendous failure. From that time on he had stuck to his principle of pretending a comedy was a tragedy and a tragedy a comedy, and he was assured of success on each occasion. Because he had become so famous in the meantime that he could afford to do almost anything he wanted, the court, to which he had been summoned by the aggrieved theatergoer, acquitted him because he had called the theatergoer just as stupid as all the other theatergoers in the world, who are numbered in the millions. After the proceedings the playwright maintained that the presiding judge had acquitted him because he, the presiding judge, hated the theater and everything connected with it more than anything else in the world, which he, the playwright, could well understand because that was his own feeling.

An author who had written only one play, which he would allow to
be performed on only one occasion in what in his opinion was the
best theater in the world and, likewise, only directed by, in his
opinion, the best director and acted by the best actors in the world,
had installed himself, before the curtain rose on the first night, in
a seat in the gallery that was best suited to his purpose but was
invisible to the audience, had sighted his machine gun, specially constructed for the purpose by the Swiss firm of Vetterli, and, after the
curtain had risen, had put a bullet through the head of every member
of the audience who had, in his opinion, laughed in the wrong place.
At the end of the performance only those members of the audience
whom he had shot, and who were therefore dead, remained seated in
the theater. The actors and the theater manager had not allowed
themselves to be disturbed for a moment by the self-willed author
and the events he had perpetrated.

A woman in Atzbach was murdered by her husband because, in his opinion, she had carried the wrong child with her to safety from their burning house. She had not saved their eight-year-old son, for whom the man had special plans, but had saved their daughter, who was not loved by the husband. When the husband was asked, in the District Court in Wels, what plans he had had for his son, who had been completely consumed by the fire, the husband replied that he had intended him to be an anarchist and a mass murderer of dictatorships and thus a destroyer of the state.

Presence of mind was displayed by a man in Rutzenmoos who saved a three-year-old boy from a mad bull, as the *Linzer Tagblatt* reports. The man, a cement worker employed by the firm of Hatschek, which has for decades furnished employment to thousands of workers and is constantly showing examples of civic-mindedness in the whole area by building children's homes and hospitals and giving financial support to old-people's homes and lunatic asylums, is said to have diverted the bull's attention from the boy with a bright red cardigan. The boy managed to get up and run away while the bull rushed at the man and mauled him so terribly that he died the following day in the Vöcklabruck emergency hospital that had been founded by the firm of Hatschek. The *Linzer Tagblatt* writes of the fortunate circumstance that the cement worker from Rutzenmoos happened to be wearing the red cardigan that his wife had knitted him for Christmas at precisely the moment at which the bull attacked the boy and had been able to turn the bull's attention *away* from the boy and to himself. At the cement worker's funeral, hundreds of his colleagues were present, and, in the nature of things, as on all such occasions, the management of the firm of Hatschek was there in full force, not to speak of the rest of the population, which always likes to go to such funerals as they substitute for the lack of a local theater with its constant first nights. Today the *Linzer Tagblatt* has a picture of the boy from Rutzenmoos, a picture of the rescuer's wife, a picture of the red cardigan that the woman had knitted her husband for Christmas, a picture of the site where the event occurred, and a picture of the bull whose attention had been drawn by the Rutzenmoos cement worker away from the boy from Rutzenmoos and to the cement worker from Rutzenmoos. The vicious bull has, as the *Linzer Tagblatt* writes, been slaughtered.

To our horror, the very neighbor whom we had for decades thought of as the best natured and hardest working and, we always thought, the most contented of all our neighbors has turned out to be a murderer. The man, a foreman in a zinc foundry in Vorchdorf, who left home every morning at six o'clock and returned from Vorchdorf every evening at six o'clock to spend the evening with his wife and two children and of whom even the fire department, to which, in the nature of things, he has belonged since he was ten, spoke only in terms of the highest praise, as did the parish priest, who had often inveigled him into doing repairs in the church, free of charge of course, murdered a so-called mesmerist who lived near Vorchdorf and was widely known and liked, because, when he broke into the room of her house on the main road in which he supposed he would find the money that the mesmerist and lay healer had collected from her clientele over time and stashed away, she surprised him in the act. Our neighbor told the police that he had wanted to supplement his income because the zinc foundry paid him too little.

At the end of the war some German soldiers were living in a disused cement silo near Steinbach am Ziehberg. Before the Americans arrived, they withdrew from the silo and bolted and barred the silo from the outside. When, a few days ago, the owner of the silo opened the entrance to the silo, which had totally rusted out, with a heavy stonebreaker's hammer, intending to demolish the old silo that had been in disuse for so long and to use the land to build an establishment for breeding and fattening pigs, he made a grisly discovery. Just inside the entrance to the silo were two totally decayed human bodies still wearing German uniform trousers and so-called army shirts. The farmer ascertained that they must have been comrades of the German soldiers who were living in the silo at the end of the war and who disappeared overnight. The authorities immediately tried to inform the relatives of the two men who had died in the silo. Even after thirty-two years, the papers of the two men who were found in the silo were so well preserved that there was not the slightest difficulty in deciphering them. One man was a lieutenant, the other a private first-class. Both were from Nackenheim on the Rhine. The question now is whether their former comrades, who are possibly still alive, should be traced or not. People are asking themselves whether the two were intentionally or unintentionally left behind in the firmly bolted and barred silo. In any case, a crime cannot be ruled out, in their opinion.

A famous surgeon and university professor, immediately after cutting short an operation that was not in itself difficult because he had suddenly lost his nerve and had to leave the completion of the operation to his assistant, was then not frank about it, either to the public or to the patient when she had regained consciousness, insofar as he was not honest enough to admit the real facts of the case but permitted the patient to congratulate him on the success of the operation. Not to speak of the excessively valuable gifts, including a gold pocket watch that Napoleon I is supposed to have worn, which he accepted from his patient without more ado. We do not know how many famous surgeons lose their nerve every day and cut short operations and leave their assistants to continue the operations and then permit themselves to be congratulated and showered with presents, but their number is supposed to be almost as great as the number of famous surgeons. And the number of unknown and unthanked assistants who can never allow themselves to lose their nerve is just as high. We have always preferred to be operated on by the assistants of famous surgeons who are also always famous medical professors, and not by these surgeons and professors themselves. And we have always come out of it very well and alive.

As long as doctors in hospitals are interested only in bodies and not in the soul, of which apparently they know next to nothing, we are bound to call hospitals institutions not only of public law but also of public murder and to call the doctors murderers and their accomplices. After a so-called amateur scholar from Ottnang am Hausruck, who had been admitted to the Vöcklabruck hospital because of a so-called *curious condition*, had been given a thorough physical examination, he had asked—as he states in a letter to the medical journal *Der Arzt* (The Doctor)—*And what about my soul?* To which the doctor who had been examining his body replied, Be quiet!

A certain Princess Radziwil, with whom, on several occasions, I took an evening stroll along the Vistula near Warsaw, told me of an uncle of hers who had retired to his castle near Radom on his fiftieth birthday because he had sworn on his twenty-first birthday that he would do so. Friends who had thought he would not recall this oath after thirty years, or would simply ignore it, were therefore very surprised when on the day after his fiftieth birthday he spent the night in Radom and swore he would never leave Radom again. As the time apparently began to drag in Radom while he was waiting for his death, he shot himself on his fifty-first birthday. When I asked the princess why her uncle had acted in this way, she said her uncle had once said to her that having to live for fifty years in this world, without, when all's said and done, being asked, is more than enough for any thoughtful man. Anyone who goes on living after that is either weak in the *head* or is a weak *character*.

A certain Prince Potocki, a nephew of the famous Potocki who wrote the Saragossa manuscript and in so doing ensured himself a permanent niche in world literature, is said to have closed all the shutters on his estate in the neighborhood of Kazimierz, one after the other and from top to bottom, and, after once more making sure that all the shutters in his castle were really shut, he apparently put a bullet through his head over a copy of Goethe's *Faust* that was open at exactly the place where the Easter promenade comes to an end. The prince is said to have drawn a red line under the end of the Easter promenade before committing suicide and to have placed a question mark beneath it. In his will he expressed the wish that the shutters, which, as he expressly stated in the will, he had shut for thirty years, should not be opened until thirty years after his death. The Potocki family honored his wishes. Immediately after the Potockis had reopened the shutters, they sold the castle near Kazimierz.

The satirist Lec, who was a good friend of mine until his death and in whose house I was a guest on several occasions and who always wrote his philosophical-satirical statements in what he called his wife's cook-books, insisted, every time I walked with him across a particular stretch of the so-called Nowy Swiat about hundred meters long and thirty wide—and whenever I was in Warsaw I would walk along the Nowy Swiat with him almost every day—that the most dangerous opponents of the regime then in power were buried beneath this stretch and that he himself had witnessed the way in which those who were in power at the present day had murdered their opponents and buried them at this spot. When I asked people what they had to say about Lec's claim, I was always confronted with head-shaking and left without an answer. But Lec always spoke the truth.

In Cracow, in which, as is well known, communism has held sway since the end of the so-called Second World War, there was a man who, whenever he visited the so-called royal vault on the Wawel, always heard the royal hymn coming from the sarcophagus of the last Polish king. Without considering the consequences he did not, in the nature of things, immediately report this experience, which was repeated every time he entered the royal vault, but told the story in the city only after some time had passed and he had had the experience almost a hundred times. When, as a result, more and more inhabitants of Cracow and, as time passed, hundreds and thousands of them made a pilgrimage to the royal vault and to the Wawel in order to hear the royal hymn from the sarcophagus as the man had done, and hundreds and thousands of them did hear the royal hymn just as the man had, the Cracow police arrested the man and threw him into prison. The inhabitants of Cracow were forbidden, on pain of punishment, to walk along the Wawel, and the royal vault was closed. For years, anyone walking along the Wawel was subjected to a thorough interrogation by the police. Today, the royal vault on the Wawel has long since been reopened and no one remembers the affair.

At a reception given by the German ambassador in Lisbon, the former king of Italy, Umberto, in quite a long conversation with the communist leader Cunhal, kept paying him compliments, while Cunhal, for his part, was always kind enough to open the door for the former king or to draw up an armchair for him. It was as though I had, throughout the evening, been witness to a thoroughly friendly conversation in which the former monarch was constantly praising communist world revolution, and the communist leader was constantly praising the achievements of the monarchy. Finally, Umberto invited Cunhal to visit him at his house in Sintra, the most charming and, indeed, the most beautiful spot in Portugal, and Cunhal accepted the invitation. In the middle of the night, on my way home through Lisbon, the clamor of the angry crowds was a perverse political contradiction.

In Portugal, dogs that have been killed or have simply died are not buried as they are in our country, but decompose and shrivel up in the open. In the Alentejo region, for example, they lie there, if they are even dragged off the street, on the left and right of the streets with their legs splayed and their tails rigid. We met smart farmers who throw dead dogs under their orange trees, which then always bear at least twice as much fruit as the others.

At the University of Coimbra, where I had been invited to give a lecture, a professor of the history of law with whom I was having dinner in a small wine bar after my lecture said that on the day of the so-called *First Revolution* all the members of his faculty had been hanged in the university's so-called natural history room because they refused to declare their solidarity with the revolutionaries of the day. Two years later, on the day of the so-called *Second Revolution*, those who had hanged his colleagues two years earlier were hanged in the very same natural history room. In answer to my question as to why he himself was still alive, he replied that he had *foreseen* everything that he had related to me—and which was actually true—*in a dream*. He knew that the dream he had had a year before the actual occurrences would become reality and had accepted an invitation, arranged for him by a friend who had been teaching there for some years, to teach for four years in England at the University of Oxford. In the nature of things, he said, he found it depressing that he was still alive and teaching at the University of Coimbra, but he had long since come to terms with this constant depression.

DECISION

According to careful estimates, in the last earthquake to strike Bucharest, 2,500 people lost their lives; exact calculations, however, have shown that some 4,000 people perished beneath the ruins. This number would have been reduced by 500 if the city had acted contrary to the express orders of the official of the Bucharest administration responsible for these things to bulldoze the rubble of the hotel that was totally destroyed rather than to clear it away, and had actually cleared the rubble away. For a whole week after the earthquake, people could still hear the cries of hundreds of those who had been buried coming from the rubble. The official of the city administration had the area around the hotel cordoned off until he received reports that absolutely nothing more was stirring beneath the rubble and not a single sound was still to be heard from the rubble. Not until two and a half weeks after the earthquake were the people of Bucharest permitted to view the heap of rubble, which was completely bulldozed in the third week. The official is said to have refused, on grounds of expense, to rescue some 500 guests of the hotel who had been buried. Rescuing them would have cost a thousand times more than bulldozing, even without taking into account the fact that probably hundreds of severely injured people would have been brought out from the rubble who would then have had to be supported by the state for the rest of their lives. According to reports, the official had, in the nature of things, assured himself of the support of the Romanian government. His promotion to a higher position in the civil service is said to be imminent.

In the Persian Gulf we made the acquaintance of a German librarian whom the German government had, for political reasons, as he himself stated, transferred from the University of Marburg on the Lahn to a town on the Persian Gulf. We visited the librarian, of whose existence we had learned in Shiraz, where we had been living for several weeks for the purpose of studying the customs of the inhabitants of this stereotypical Persian town, in a hospital in Shiraz and were shocked at his condition. The man was almost totally paralyzed and could scarcely make himself understood. He said he had contributed an article to a learned journal published in Frankfurt attacking the German legal system and had been posted to the Persian Gulf as a result. Initially he had come to terms with the situation because he was interested in the Persian Gulf and thought he would be able to pursue scholarly studies there. But the climate in the Persian Gulf, which is truly deadly, had laid him low in a very short time and had finally destroyed his health. He maintained that his greatest mistake was entering the so-called civil service, which had meant nothing for him but his systematic destruction, first his intellectual and then his physical destruction. Anyone, he said to us, who enters the civil service, no matter for what reason and no matter in what capacity, will be laid low and destroyed. He told us that he had addressed hundreds of requests to the German government asking them to take him out of, as he expressed it to us, the hell of the Persian Gulf, but all of these requests remained unanswered. In his opinion he had quite consciously been driven to death by the state he had wanted to serve but which he had allowed himself on one single occasion to criticize. We were unable to help the librarian. Four days after our visit we learned of his death. Three weeks later, the German government, as we subsequently learned, published an obituary notice in the *Frankfurter Allgemeine Zeitung* in which it expressed its regret at the librarian's death. The civil service destroys anyone who enters it. No matter which master a person serves in the state, it is the wrong one.

In Cairo, at the end of a reception given by an attaché at the French embassy on the occasion of his wife's birthday and attended by about a hundred people who spent most of the evening talking about Baudelaire's *Fleurs du Mal*, which the host, after years of work, had translated into Egyptian, so many people were crowding in front of the elevator on the seventh floor, on which the attaché lived, that we, who had plenty of time, stepped back out of the way. When the door of the elevator had closed, the elevator—to the horror of those who had remained behind—crashed down the shaft and was smashed to pieces. Those who had remained behind were unable to move for several seconds; they stood speechless in the total silence that followed the explosion that the crash of the elevator had caused on the ground floor. Only after the first cries could be heard did they dare to venture out of their state of paralysis, but they were incapable of doing anything sensible. They did not want to go down right away, and they went back into the attaché's apartment. We, too, had gone back into the attaché's apartment because we were just as incapable as the others of going downstairs. It was not until three hours after the incident that we, along with the others, left the attaché's apartment after being told that the bodies of all those killed in the elevator had been taken away. In the nature of things, we ask ourselves to this day why we didn't push our way into the elevator and why we stepped back to let the others get on. We have heard that every year in Cairo several old elevators that are overloaded crash down the shaft.

Near the Coptic quarter in Cairo we noticed whole rows of streets in whose four- and five-story houses thousands of chickens and goats and even pigs are kept. We tried to imagine what the noise would be like if these houses were to burn down.

EXPEDITION

My grandfather's sister's husband, an unsuccessful painter in Europe who through his marriage had come into a fairly large estate, which he owed to my grandfather's industry, left at the turn of the century on—as he maintained at the time—a scientific expedition to Argentina and stopped over in some coastal city. He had announced that the duration of the expedition, and thus of his stay in South America, would be four months; he is supposed to have been involved in a scientific topic with which, without exception, all of our ancestors have been concerned and in which some of them achieved fame by their publications on precisely this topic. After the four months had passed, my great-aunt heard no more of her husband, who had, up to that point, written to Europe from time to time. One day she received, in the mail, her husband's wallet with a note saying that her husband had taken a horse in that coastal city and had ridden off and not returned. According to eyewitnesses, there were terrible storms around at the time, and it was assumed that he had died in these storms. Nor was there any sign of the horse. My grandfather's sister therefore had to come to terms with the death of her husband, who was originally from Eger, and she was left alone with the twelve-year-old daughter her husband had also abandoned. Sixty-two years after her husband had ridden off in South America and had, as she certainly believed, died, she *learned* from *Le Monde*, which she had read every day for forty years, that her husband, sixty-one years after being declared dead by the Austrian authorities, had in fact only now died in Rio de Janeiro, unmarried but surrounded by women who looked after him, and as a world-famous painter who, as *Le Monde* wrote, had given South American painting and, indeed, the whole of South American art a new impetus and an international repute, using the same name that he had lived under in Europe but with an 'o' at the end. Immediately, his widow, who had, in the meantime, grown very very old but not so old that she could not read *Le Monde* anymore, and her daughter had considered recovering by legal means what was now known to be their husband's and father's *massive estate*.

It was for the same artist whose story I have just told that my great-grandfather built a large and, by the standards of the day, sensationally equipped studio at a spot that the artist himself had been allowed to select, an eminence overlooking the Wallersee, where, for a painter, the most favorable of all light conditions prevail. With the money that the studio alone cost, as my relatives kept reiterating, they could have bought and modernized several farms. Shortly after the studio was finished, the person for whom it was built left, as I have already reported, for South America and disappeared and was declared dead, and the studio lost its true purpose. As I have often been told, it was—being an outstanding attraction in this uncultured peasant area—always marveled at, but in the end it was nonetheless allowed to fall into total disrepair. For a long time the farmers in the area, who were all related to us in one way or another, found a use for the paintings by the painter who had, for whatever reason, emigrated to South America—gigantic canvases on which he painted only his idiosyncratic notion of Jesus Christ—as tarpaulins, for which purpose, as one can well imagine, they were exceptionally well suited. Of course, these canvases were only used as tarpaulins by the farmers with the image of Christ on the *inside*.

A man from Terbinje who looked so much like the Yugoslavian president that the two could easily be mistaken for one another offered to
place himself at the disposal of the administration in Belgrade for
physically demanding duties that the president of Yugoslavia had to
undertake, not without submitting a precise list of those duties that
he, as he believed, could easily carry out in the president's stead and
which the then president seemed to him to be already much too weak
physically to undertake. It would, he said, be an honor for him to
undertake, in place of the president of the so-called People's Republic
of Yugoslavia, duties that the president was not absolutely bound to
perform, and he asked nothing for the services he was offering. Since
the man who had made Belgrade the offer three years previously has
not been seen again from that day to this, many people, not only in
Trebinje and environs but now in the whole of Yugoslavia, believe he
has already taken up his duties in the Yugoslavian capital. The people
who give voice to this supposition are labeled slanderers. Those who
claim to know that the man is in prison or in a lunatic asylum or has
long since been liquidated are similarly labeled slanderers. This would
make all Yugoslavians slanderers.

When the powerful become too powerful in their own countries and, while holding power over a long period, dissipate not only the whole national wealth but also the intellectual wealth of their state, there are still many people in many countries who are surprised when, here and there, overnight, and, in the nature of things, frequently in the most barbarous manner, those in power are assassinated and anarchy reigns. We can call it luck, said the professor from that state from which he could have fled and in which the prime minister had been assassinated the week before. When the professor returned to his own country, however, he was immediately arrested at the frontier and thrown into prison in spite of the fact that a new prime minister, and one totally opposed to the one who had been assassinated, had assumed power in the meantime.

The president of the country in Central Europe in which the president goes in fear of his life every minute of the day—and for good reason—told his confidant of a plan he had forged during hundreds of sleepless nights whereby it would be possible for the president to desert the state that he—in common with all the other presidents in eastern Europe—had brought to total ruin, and to take with him such a large fortune that he would be assured of a long and secure life of luxury in an ideally suited foreign country. He said that he wished to realize his plan as soon as possible but that it was essential for his confidant to keep absolutely quiet about the whole affair. The confidant, who had for decades enjoyed the confidence of the president, promised the president that he would remain silent, and for his part the president promised the confidant a fortune large enough to make it possible for the confidant, after he had fled, to live to the end of his days, like the president, in a carefree and truly luxurious manner. The president and his confidant had scarcely been in agreement for two minutes before the confidant simplified the whole affair by killing the president with a skillful shot through the base of the skull and proclaiming himself president. In a trice he liquidated all the supporters of his predecessor and role model and made a confidant out of the man who shot the greatest number of supporters. Since he was already aware of the perfect example of political science, he merely waited, in the nature of things, for the most favorable opportunity for getting rid of his confidant before the latter should liquidate him. But he acted too slowly.

At the end of a philosophical discussion that had tormented two professors from the University of Graz for decades and had brought not only them but also their families to total ruin and which, as they are reported to have perceptively told a third colleague one day, like all philosophical discussions led to nothing and which, finally, in the nature of things, ruined and actually drove this colleague, who had also become embroiled in their discussion, insane, the two professors from Graz, after inviting their third colleague and adversary, out of habit, so to speak, into the house they had rented jointly for the sole purpose of their philosophical discussion, had blown the house up. They had spent all the money they had left on the dynamite necessary for the purpose. Since the families of all three professors were present in the house at the time of the explosion, they had also blown up their families. The surviving relatives of one of the professors and adversaries, for whom the decades-long philosophical discussion—as they themselves had clearly demonstrated—had proved fatal, considered suing the state because they were of the opinion that the state's moral and intellectual bankruptcy had driven all three to their deaths, but they did not bring such an action after all, because they realized the futility of such an action.

Near Sulden, years ago, in a quiet inn to which I had withdrawn for several weeks so as to see as few people as possible and to have contact only with what was absolutely necessary, for which the area around Sulden is suited like no other—and it was above all for the sake of my diseased lung that I had gone to the remoteness of Sulden, which I knew from earlier days—a Herr Natter from Innsbruck, the only guest in the inn aside from myself, who stated that he had once been rector of the University of Innsbruck but had been dismissed from office because of a libelous attack and had actually been thrown into prison, though shortly thereafter his innocence had been established, told me each day what he had dreamed the previous night. In one of the dreams he told me about, he had run around to hundreds of Tirolean authorities to get permission to have his father's grave opened, but this had been denied him, whereupon he had tried to open his father's grave himself and, after hours of the most exhausting digging, had finally succeeded. He said he had wanted to see his father once more. However, when he opened the coffin and actually removed the lid, it was not his father lying in the coffin but a dead pig. As usual, Natter wanted to know, in this case as well, what his dream meant.

We spoke to a number of people in Perast from whom we sought to find out who had once owned the deserted and already almost totally ruined palaces, for we had read nothing about them. The people we spoke to merely laughed at our questions and turned their backs on us and ran away. A few kilometers down the road, in Risan, we heard that there were no more normal people living in Perast; the city had been given over to quite a large number of lunatics who could do as they liked there and were supplied with food by the state once a week.

A postman was suspended in Lend because for years he had not delivered any letter that he thought contained sad news or, in the nature of things, any of the cards announcing a death that came his way, but had burned them all in his own home. The post office finally had him committed to the lunatic asylum in Scherrnberg, where he goes around in a postman's uniform and continually delivers letters that are deposited by the asylum's administration in a letter box specially built into one of the walls of the asylum and that are addressed to his fellow patients. According to reports, the postman asked for his uniform as soon as he was committed to the lunatic asylum in Scherrnberg *so as not to be driven mad.*

A post office official who was charged with murdering a pregnant woman told the court that he did not know why he had murdered the pregnant woman but that he had murdered his victim *as carefully as possible*. In response to all the presiding judge's questions, he always used the word *carefully*, whereupon the court proceedings against him were abandoned.

The most intelligent and famous female poet that our country has produced in the present century died in a hospital in Rome from the effects of scalds and burns that she must have sustained in her bath-tub, according to the authorities. I used to go on trips with her, and on these trips I shared many of her philosophical views, as well as her views on the course of the world and the course of history, which had frightened her all her life. Many attempts on her part to return to her native Austria, however, came to grief because of the shamelessness of her female rivals and the stupidity of the Viennese authorities. The news of her death reminded me that she was the first guest in my then still completely empty house. She was always on the run and had always seen people for what they really were, as a slow-witted, stupid, thoughtless mass that one simply has to break with. Like me, she had early in life discovered the entrance to hell, and entered this hell even though there was a danger of perishing in this hell at a very early age. People are trying to decide whether her death was an accident or whether it was suicide. Those who believe in the poet's suicide keep saying that she was broken by herself, whereas in reality and in the nature of things she was broken by her environment and, at bottom, by the meanness of her homeland, which persecuted her at every turn even when she was abroad, just as it does so many others.

In the past few months, three former classmates of mine have committed suicide; they were all friends of mine and kept me company with their arts for almost the whole of my life and were the ones who really made my existence in the least bit possible. The musician killed (shot) himself because people had no ear for his art. The painter killed (hanged) himself because people had no eyes for his art. The scientist, with whom I even went to primary school, killed (poisoned) himself because people, in his opinion, had no head for science. All three had had to withdraw from life because they were in despair over the fact that the world no longer had the feelings or abilities to take in their art and their science.

As the reason for his brother's suicide, a doctor in Wels—with whom I once went to primary school and who was compelled by the practice of medicine increasingly to abandon his intellectual and artistic talents as he became absorbed in his profession as a total speculation in the human body—suggested that his brother had suffered all his life from having come to know a person he described as a highly talented female musician and concert pianist who gradually *op*pressed and finally *sup*-pressed his talents, which were really extraordinary, which reminded me of that unfortunate genius, Robert Schumann.

Our respect for a writer whom we never in our life dared approach was without doubt at its peak when we stayed in the same hotel in which the writer whom we admired had been living for some time, and were introduced on the hotel terrace one day—through the good offices of a friend—to the man we admired. We can remember no better example of the fact that to approach actually means nothing more than to withdraw. The closer we came to our writer after the first meeting, the more we distanced ourselves from him—and with the same intensity—and the more we got to know his personality, the more we distanced ourselves from his works; every word he spoke to us, every thought he thought about us, distanced us from that same word and that same thought in his works. He finally disgusted us totally, took us apart, dissolved us, and put us back together again. When we left the hotel—and the only thing that made us happy about that was that we could still make do without the writer—we had the impression that the writer had destroyed his personality in our eyes just as he had his work. The author of those hundreds of thoughts and ideas and perceptions, whom we had served for decades with our understanding and to whom we had been loyal in our love, had, by not refusing our acquaintance but ultimately by seeking it against our will, destroyed his works. Whenever we heard his name after that, we were repelled.

In Vienna, where lack of consideration and impudence towards thinkers and artists has always been greater than anywhere else, and which can assuredly be called the graveyard of imagination and ideas, and where thousands more geniuses go to the dogs and are destroyed than actually come to light and achieve fame and international fame, a man was found dead in a hotel in the inner city who with complete lucidity had written a note stating the reason for his suicide and had pinned this note to his jacket. For decades, he wrote, he had pursued an idea and was actually able to realize and bring this idea—in the nature of things a philosophical one—to a conclusion in a moderately long work, but his powers had finally been completely devoured by the idea. The appreciation he had nonetheless expected was not forthcoming. Although he had finally *begged* to be appreciated, the institutions and people competent to give him this appreciation had denied it him. His pointing to the immensity of his work had done no good. It was not only his colleagues' jealousy but the whole anti-intellectual atmosphere that pervaded the city—its mindless lack of humanity—that had driven him to his death. However, as he did not wish to betray his own character, he had burned his opus before he died, he had burned his life's work and actually reduced it to nothing within the space of a few minutes after taking decades to bring it to fruition, but he had not wanted to leave it to a posterity that was in no way worthy of it. The terrible idea that he, like so many of his fellows, would be appreciated only after his death and would thus be exploited and become famous was what had caused him to destroy what he had achieved, which was really of much greater value than anything that had been thought of or written in his field. The city of Vienna, and this is how he ended what he had written in the note, has lived since its founding on the works of its geniuses who have committed suicide; he was not minded to become another link in this chain of geniuses.

Not long ago it became known that a high school student collapsed on the so-called Floridsdorf bridge after walking back and forth across the Floridsdorf bridge about a thousand times. He stated that on the way to school he had been seized by, as he put it, a *terrible fear of school*, which would not let him leave the bridge once he had set foot on it and compelled him to walk back and forth across it almost a thousand times. To take his mind off his fear, he said, he had counted the number of steps he took as he went back and forth across the Floridsdorf bridge, but he had finally given up this distraction because it was too much for him. He had, however, at least been able to *count and take note* of how often he had gone one way and how often the other across the Floridsdorf bridge. Exactly nine hundred ninety-eight times. His parents fetched the exhausted sixteen-year-old from a police station in the so-called Floridsdorfer Spitz, where police officers had taken him. What more will happen to him cannot be said.

If the newspapers in this country bother to say anything about an outstanding artist who was born in their country and who is already of international importance and enjoys international fame, they always talk about a *certain* artist, because in this way they can do him much greater harm in his native land than if they were simply to write down what they really and truly think of this artist, who, because he comes from their own land and belongs to their generation—which has not produced much that is notable—incurs their hatred as nothing else on earth does and is pursued by their hatred to the end of his life and theirs. They never forgive him for giving up on them, at a certain point, for the sake of his art and his science and for continually demonstrating his greatness and their pettiness with work that was always at the cutting edge. If they cannot avoid writing about this—in their opinion—common renegade because the rest of the world is writing about him, they do so, but only in order to drag down into the mire the man they have been persecuting all his life. They do not notice that in so doing they themselves sink deeper and deeper into the mire. With their envy and their hatred they drove my friend to Newcastle in Australia, where he sacrificed himself for his science. When, tormented with homesickness, he told me years ago that he was going to leave Newcastle and return to his native land, I immediately sent him a telegram warning him about returning to his native land, drawing his attention to the fact that this native land was, in truth, nothing more than a common hell in which the intellect is incessantly defamed and art and science are destroyed and that his return would mean his end. He did not follow my advice. He is a terminally ill man, for whom the lunatic asylum *am Steinhof* has for years been his regular though hideous dwelling place.